TO BE CHOSEN

DAKIARA

MIND FLOW PUBLISHING & PRODUCTION LLC

CONTENTS

This is a work of fiction. Names, characters, businesses, places, events, locales, and incidents are either the products of the author's imagination or used in a fictious manner. Any resemblances to actual persons, living or dead, or actual events is purely coincidental.

First Printing: 2020

ISBN 978-1-951271-15-2 Paperback

ISBN 978-1-951271-14-5 Ebook

Additional copies of this book and others are available by mail or by visiting the website listed below. Check website for pricing.

Mind Flow Publishing & Production LLC

PO Box 48768 Cumberland, North Carolina 28331-8768

www.mindflowpublishingproduction.com

Cover design by Carrie & Co.

Editing by Stories Matter Editing

Formatting Design by Clarity Townsend

Thank you for helping to bring "To Be Chosen" to life...

CHAPTER ONE

FALLEN

$\mathcal{G}$abriel Mendoza had never thought he would stoop this low. But he was starving, and the night was cold. He could have found a shelter but that would have taken ages to find one that wasn't already at maximum capacity. He needed something just for a few hours and he needed it quickly.

Who was going to care if he snuck into some rich guy's pool house to sleep and eat whatever he had in the minibar? They did not need it anyway. No one needed two houses especially when there were people like Gabriel who didn't even have a stable place to sleep.

Gabriel stared up at the house. He had been frozen in place for the last fifteen minutes contemplating his options. He knew exactly what he wanted to do but his feet were planted firmly on the ground. Every time he thought of moving it felt like a stone was dropped into his legs only making them heavier.

He had never done anything like this before, just small petty crimes like stealing chips from a shop. The worse thing he had ever done was get drunk and start a bar fight. His mother had drilled it into his head for years before her death that if he had done something illegal it would send him to Hell. He didn't really believe in things like that but now her voice was coming back to him.

"Baby boy, you have to promise me that you will be a good boy..."

Gabriel squeezed his eyes shut. He needed to do this. His mother would understand. She would not want him to be out on the streets like he was. He was not hurting anyone.

That is what he kept reminding himself at least. No one was being hurt. He would be out before anyone noticed he was even there. All he had to do was take the first step.

"Come on, Gabriel," he muttered through chattering teeth. He was sure parts of him were already turning blue by now. As he adjusted the strap on his bag he glanced up and down the street. Someone was heading his way.

He cursed under his breath before pushing himself forward. As much as he hated the idea of breaking the law, he hated the idea of getting caught in the act even more. If he were arrested again, he did not think the judge would go easy on him. He quickly pressed himself against the fence and pulled his hood further down.

Two people passed by him as he watched from the shadows. They were talking loudly about a band and were obviously drunk. Even if they did see him, they probably would not care. Then again, he was a poor kid lurking around in the shadows in the rich part of town. They would definitely find it suspicious.

Gabriel stayed pressed against the fence until the two people turned the corner at the end of the street. Carefully, he stepped back onto the sidewalk and looked up at the house. "Okay," he whispered. "I have to do this now."

"Don't do anything I wouldn't do..." his mother's voice called out into his head again.

"Sorry Mama," Gabriel whispered. He stepped back into the street before taking a running jump towards the fence.

He used the momentum to kick off the fence and jumped up so he could grab the top of it. He cursed as his hand hit the top, the wooden ends came to a point, but didn't stop. He pulled himself over. As gracefully as he could he dropped down to the other side. Thankfully, he landed on his feet and only stumbled a little.

He grinned and then held his hands straight up. "And he stuck the landing, the crowd is going wild," he whispered. He then looked down at his hand and poked the small cut that was barely bleeding.

After a moment to put himself back together he nodded. "Okay," he mumbled and glanced towards the pool house. It was so dark he could barely see two feet in front of him. He started walking towards the pool house, clutching the strap of his bag.

He bit his lip as he knocked into a chair then stumbled to the side and knocked into another chair. As he tried to move away from the chairs, he hit the table and it screeched against the stone patio.

Gabriel froze and squeezed his eyes shut. His vision narrowed down to a point and he listened for any kind of noise that meant the owners were awake.

He waited for ten minutes before slowly pulling away from the table. He took in a deep breath and stood up straight before he started to head towards the pool house again.

"Don't do this..."

Gabriel shook his mother's voice away. He had to think

rationally and not let his dead mother rule over everything he did.

When he was walking, he noticed that there was a light on in the house that was not on before. How had he not noticed it turning on? He was such an idiot.

Then someone came in front of the window with a phone to his ear. Gabriel's eyes went wide when he looked right at him.

In a flash he turned on his heel to start running. But he did not realize that he was seconds away from stepping into the pool and as he went to push off to start running his foot slipped into the pool. He tried to get up, but his foot got caught on the tarp that covered the pool and he fell backwards.

Instantly he felt ice cold water surround him. He struggled against the tarp as he tried to swim up to the surface.

Once he broke free, he was shaking violently but did not stop moving. He could see blue and red flashing lights coming from the front of his house. He had to get out of there as quickly as he could. He took in a deep breath and bolted towards the fence.

As soon as he landed on the other side of the fence a light was flashed on him. His eyes went wide and froze like a deer caught in the headlights. He shook his head and started to run in the other direction. He was not going to get caught. Not again. Not like this.

The police gave chase as soon as they saw him running. "Stop running!" one of the officers called.

Gabriel glanced over his shoulder before shaking his head. He pushed himself to run faster but the water on his skin was not helping. It made the air sting as it lashed against his skin. That didn't stop him though.

The officer shook his head and ran as fast as he could. He

chased after Gabriel until he finally caught up to him. He snatched the back of his sweatshirt and pulled him back.

A choking noise escaped Gabriel and his hands flew to his throat before he was pulled to the ground. The hood of his sweatshirt was still balled up in the officer's hand choking him. He quickly put up his hands, shaking. "I'm sorry," he cried, choking on the words. "I'm sorry. I won't run anymore."

The officer dug his knee into his back before cuffing him. "Not like you have much of a choice anymore," he laughed. He looked up as his partner finally reached them. "About time. Help me get him to the car."

He hauled Gabriel up by the cuffs making them dig hard against his wrists and cut into him. He shot a dirty look to him when the young man whimpered. "Quite complaining," he hissed. He grabbed one of his arms while his partner grabbed the other and they dragged him back to the cruiser.

They tossed Gabriel in the back and shut the door. The young man groaned as he sat up. He looked over the back seat and gagged at the smell of it. Someone had definitely thrown up in there recently.

They started driving away and all he could picture was his mother's disappointed face. He closed his eyes and leaned his head back against the hard cushion. "Sorry, Mom," he whispered.

Gabriel stood in front of the judge drumming his fingers anxiously against the table. He closed his eyes and patiently waited for his attorney to show up. He was still a bit battered and bruised from the night of the arrest but the bruise around his neck was starting to fade. The cuts on his wrists from where the cuffs dug into him were still raw and they pulled every time he moved his hands.

"Mr. Mendoza," the judge called. "Your lawyer was supposed to be here twenty minutes ago. Where is she?"

Gabriel looked up at the judge before looking out into the crowd. He could see the two men whose yard he broke into. He looked away quickly when he caught their eye. "I don't know Your Honor. She was supposed to speak with me yesterday but...but she never showed up. I don't know where she is. The court appointed her to me. I didn't...I didn't do anything."

"If your lawyer does not show up within the next five minutes, I will have to sentence you without one," he informed him sternly.

"Sir, I don't think you can do that," Gabriel said. "I...I need a lawyer. If..."

"Mr. Mendoza, we have provided you with a lawyer, but you have to make sure you get in contact with them. I'm sure you're well aware that this is..." he looked at the papers in front of him, "your fifth offense. The chances of you going to prison are very high."

Gabriel heard a muffled good from the audience and he let out a small sigh. "Yes, Your Honor, I just don't understand why I have to- "

"Sorry Your Honor," A woman said as she rushed into the courtroom. She wore a confident smile despite showing up almost twenty minutes late. "I thought I was scheduled with a different Mendoza today. One hundred percent my fault."

Gabriel turned and was shocked at what he saw.

A woman with long dark brown hair tied up into a bun, taller than him, and too beautiful for the job she was in. He could have sworn she was an actress playing in a movie. Then again, if this was a movie then he wouldn't feel like he was about to be locked away in a dark corner for the rest of his natural born life.

"Ah," the judge said, looking down at the papers again. "Miss Harp, right?"

"Yes, Your Honor," Dani said with a grin. She pushed open the swinging gate that separated the defendant's table from the spectators' seats and walked over to Gabriel's table. She offered him a smile.

Gabriel wanted to be angry at her but when she smiled at him, he could not hold it on for longer. Up close she was even more beautiful. She had soft looking skin and a perfect smile. There was a certain twinkle in her green eyes that made him feel like maybe it would not be that bad.

"I was wondering Your Honor, if I could have a word with my client before we continue?" she told the judge.

"No," the judge said firmly. "We haven't even started. You had a chance to speak with your client and you elected not to take it. We will begin immediately as we are already behind on the docket for the day...I have other cases to get through."

Dani looked at Gabriel and offered him a smile. "Don't worry, I've got this," she assured him.

Gabriel felt the blood drain out of his face and turned forward. It didn't matter how beautiful she was, he was still going to prison.

Twenty minutes later Gabriel was sitting there listening as Dani was finishing up with her closing remarks. "And finally, after my client was in cuffs and ready to go with the cops the two officers in question decided to manhandle him resulting in injuries to his wrist. My client is a young man who is down on his luck and is simply trying to make his life better. I understand that he has had prior arrests, but all but one was for means of survival and he was found not to be the one at fault for the fight and only was defending himself. None of that means that the police officers of this city have any right to physically abuse the people they are arresting.

Gabriel Mendoza should not be charged with breaking and entering. If anything, he should get a small slap on the wrist for trespassing."

Gabriel nearly jumped when Dani grabbed his hand and lifted it up. He gave her a confused look before looking at the judge.

"He and I think that punishment was already administrated by your officers," she finished. She set his hand back down. "I rest my case."

Five minutes later Gabriel walked out of the courtroom with all charges dropped. He couldn't believe it. He was free. No prison. He turned to his lawyer and took her hand, giving it quick shake. "Thank you, Miss Harp. I can't tell you enough how much I appreciate all your help," he told her quickly.

Dani let out a small laugh and shook her head. "It's my job to help those in need," she told him. "Can I interest you in a cup of coffee?"

Gabriel bit his lip. "I don't have the money for…"

"I'll buy it, come on," she said with a smile. "I would like to get to know the client I just defended."

Gabriel chuckled before following her. "Wait, how did you know all of that stuff? I didn't think it was in the report…"

"It wasn't in the report," Dani told him as they walked down the hall of the courthouse. "I'll tell you once we get to the coffee shop."

Gabriel gave her a small nod and stuck his hands into his pockets. "Well, no matter how you knew, thank you for fighting for me. I don't think I ever had a lawyer who actually cared."

Dani gave him another perfect smile. "Well, like I said, it's my job to help those in need."

They walked out of the courthouse and Gabriel shivered against the brisk wind. The tall buildings around them did nothing but trap the wind inside. There wasn't a far walk down the street, but it felt like ages before they finally reached the door.

"Quite a cold day, isn't it," Dani laughed. She held her jacket shut as the wind tried to blow it open and she grabbed and then pulled the door open. "Get inside before you're whisked away. You're too light to be out in weather like this."

Gabriel rolled his eyes before walking inside. When she was not looking, he looked down at himself and poked a finger against his ribs. "Can I get anything?" he asked.

"Anything. I doubt the food they gave you at the jail was any good," she chuckled. She leaned over the counter and told the barista her order before stepping back and letting Gabriel give his order.

Soon they were both tucked into a booth together and Gabriel was swallowing down his breakfast sandwich. "Okay," he said in between bites, "so are you going to tell me how you knew all of that stuff without asking me or reading it in a report. Were you in those guys' house that night and I didn't know about it?"

Dani laughed softly and shook her head. "No, no, of course not," she said. She took a sip of her coffee before making a face. "They never put in enough sugar. I always tell them I need some extra sugar in it because I definitely am not sweet enough."

Gabriel raised his eyebrow and wiped grease from his chin. "Then how did you know?" he asked softly.

She flicked two sugar packets before tearing off the top. She looked up at him as she poured them in. "Well...I guess I should start by properly introducing myself. I'm Dani Harp. I'm an angel sent from God."

9

CHAPTER TWO

WITH GRACE

*D*ani Harp knew she was falling behind in work, but she didn't think she was so far behind that she needed help. But here she was staring down at a folder open on her desk with a picture of a guy named Gabriel Mendoza.

On top of the folder was a note that said, *'Don't mess this up- G'*

After a few days of sulking around she saw the folder sitting on a stack of other folders that she needed to get through. She could have sworn she stuck it in the bottom drawer of her desk and locked it up tight.

Then again, if God wanted something done, he would be persistent, and she knew that no lock could stop him. The locks were mostly to stop Jophiel from stealing candies she usually always had in one of her desk drawers, she had an infamous sweet tooth.

Dani stared at the folder before giving in. She picked it up and brought it over to her seat. She fell into it and the chair rolled backwards a bit. She grabbed the edge of her desk and pulled herself back to it.

"Okay Gabriel Mendoza let's see what you're like," she mumbled as she started reading the first page. "Nineteen, five foot seven, thin as a twig…what does he eat? Bread and water?"

Gabriel's entire life was inside the folder. All the way from when he was first born, to him breaking his leg in the second grade, his dad leaving when he was thirteen, trying alcohol for the first time, his mother lecturing him with tears streaming down her face, and finally ending at him getting arrested for breaking and entering.

She read over the last few years of his life a few times and wondered if God had chosen the wrong person. He seemed so unrighteous. How was he supposed to help in God's work? Especially something as big as miracle work.

She kept reading and rereading it, trying to find the answer to it all. She knew that she was in no place to judge and she was not, but miracle work was done by those who were pure at heart.

When she flipped to the page that said when she was supposed to meet him and noticed that it was that day. A few hours ago, to be exact.

Dani snagged the photo of Gabriel out of the folder and quickly left her desk and started towards the door that led to Earth. To use it a badge needed to be swiped and the travel code that was in the folder had to be entered. Then it would open to the location that was needed and anyone could step out into it without alerting any humans that something heavenly had transpired.

As she walked her clothes changed into ones that a lawyer would wear. She stuck Gabriel's photo between her lips as she quickly did up her hair. She looked a mess, but it would have to do on such short notice.

"Running late?" another angel asked as she passed.

"They really need to put dates at the beginning of the folder and not the end," she called, turning around to look at them as she kept briskly walking. "I think it would save me a lot of time."

"Or you could just read the file as soon as you get the folder," he laughed.

Dani shrugged her shoulders and turned around. She reached the door and slid her badge in the keypad. It flashed red. "Come on," she muttered. She swiped it again, and the red light came on again. She quickly rubbed the badge against her leg before running it through again.

It flashed green.

A triumphant grin split her face as she quickly put in the numbers and opened the door.

She wasn't expecting to walk into a full courtroom, when she read the file it had said that it would be a small case but a hard one to get him out of.

"Sorry Your Honor," Dani said, giving them all a nervous smile. She made her way up front as quickly as she could, glancing at Gabriel when he looked back at her just to make sure she was standing at the right table.

Black hair, deep brown eyes, scar that curved around the edge of his eye, a ton of freckles, and tanned skin. Definitely the right person.

"I thought I was scheduled with a different Mendoza today. One hundred percent my fault."

After saving Gabriel from serving a year in prison Dani knew she was going to have to do something to keep him in her sights so she could tell him about her work and explain who she was.

At the trial she had started to understand why God may have wanted her to work with Gabriel. He was not such a bad guy. In fact, he looked like he wouldn't hurt anyone if he didn't have to, but she read a lot of things in his file that would contradict that.

It wasn't that he was a criminal, despite having been arrested several times before, it was that he seemed angry about something. She had figured that it was his dad leaving at first, or maybe his mother dying at such a young age, but that didn't add up to the life he chose to lead.

They were sitting in the café, Dani was taking a small sip at her drink to see if they made it right, when Gabriel asked her the question that she wasn't sure she wanted to answer yet.

"Okay," he muttered after he swallowed the large bite he just took, "so are you going to tell me how you knew all of that stuff without asking me or reading it in the report. Were you in those guys' house that night and I didn't know about it?"

Dani laughed at the question and assured him that she was not. Then she explained to him how no coffee place ever made her drink right and poured in more sugar.

She was stalling because she wasn't sure if she wanted to tell Gabriel about recruiting him to help her do her work. She knew she could do it on her own. She had been doing it for decades. It wasn't like she had just gotten her wings and needed help. She was a full-fledged angel. Dani was one of the few who just happened to have been born into the life of an Angel. Her parents before her served as Angels for many years. It was not only her duty but her honour to have been chosen for this task. Just because one is born into this life, it does not give them a free pass to stay and serve. There are tests that all Angels must go through to ensure they are the right one for this job. The tests are catered to everyone's special abilities, instead of one test fits all.

Gabriel asked again and she knew she could not keep

avoiding the question. She sighed and rubbed her forehead. She poured in more sugar before finally finding the right words to answer with.

"Well...I guess I should start by properly introducing myself. I'm Dani Harp. I'm an angel sent from God."

Gabriel stared at her, unbelievingly. He had been given a crackpot lawyer. "How did I escape prison time?" he muttered and sat back. He ran a hand over his face before laughing wryly. Of course, he would be given the lawyer that apparently was also crazy.

Dani frowned as she watched him. "Because I pled your case in a way that made you out to be the victim. Which, in a way you were."

"Damn right I was," Gabriel muttered. He finished his sandwich before grabbing his cup. "That cop didn't need to attack me the way he did."

"You're right, he didn't," Dani sighed, tucking hair that fell into her face behind her ear. "But that's not the issue we have to deal with right r`now. I've been sent here—"

"Nope," Gabriel muttered, putting up a hand to stop her. "I don't want to hear it. I'm honestly not in the mood to talk to some crazy person about their delusions. How did you even become a lawyer?"

Dani let her shoulders slump and she stared at him for a moment. "I'm not delusional. I'm honestly an angel. I've got credentials and everything."

"Credentials?" Gabriel asked with a laugh. He shook his head. "Last time I checked angels didn't carry around business cards that announced they were angels."

"I'm sure the last time you read about angels of any kind they also weren't the holy ones either," she told him, trying to keep the snarl out of her voice. "Also, a lot has changed since the bible was written. We change just like the times do. We can't stay mired in the stone age forever."

Gabriel rolled his eyes and stood up. "Well, thanks for the coffee," he told her, "and the sandwich. I don't think I'm going to stick around much longer. Don't get me wrong, I'm really grateful for you helping me out back there but I'm thinking you should probably quit being a lawyer before you mess up someone's life."

He turned and left the café before Dani even had a chance to get up and stop him.

Dani had contemplating returning to Heaven and telling God herself that the kid was a lost cause. She knew that wouldn't be right, but she didn't want to chase him all around the city only to have him keep thinking she was a lunatic. It sounded like a waste of time compared to what she could be doing.

She knew though, that if she returned to heaven without having gotten Gabriel's help, she would have all of God's wrath brought down upon her. Even if she managed to finish the stack of miracles that she allowed to pile up.

As she walked down the street, mulling over her options, it started to snow. She looked up at the sky, watching the fat flakes fall gracefully to the ground before letting out a sigh. "Why do you always insist on being dramatic?" she muttered. Then a giant gust of wind blew her in the opposite direction she was walking. No one else around her was moving and she glared back up towards the sky with a narrowed gaze. "Fine, fine. I'll get the kid."

She turned around and started walking in the direction of where Gabriel was. The way she was able to know his location, or his general location, was through a feeling she had in her chest. Almost like the hot and cold game kids played. When she got closer her chest would feel warmer and would only stop if she could actively see who she was looking for or interacting with them in some way, as she got further though it felt like ice was forming in her chest.

It took Dani an hour to finally find him. Or she hoped it was him. If it wasn't then she would feel bad for stealing a blanket from a homeless man in the middle of a snowstorm. She reached down and snagged the edge of the blanket and then as quickly as she could she tugged it off.

Gabriel sat up as quickly as he could, his hands coming up to defend himself. "Don't touch me!" he shouted.

"I'm not going to," she told him, looking him over. He already looked like he was turning blue. "Get up and follow me."

As soon as he recognized her, he snatched his blanket back. "Leave me alone," he hissed before pulling the blanket over him again. "I'm not in the mood to be murdered by some lunatic who thinks she's an angel."

"I am an angel; how do you think I found you?" she asked.

"I don't know," Gabriel muttered under the thin fabric. "You probably followed me here."

Dani rolled her eyes and pulled the blanket off of him. "Get up or you're going to die tonight."

Gabriel glared at her. "Is that a threat now? It's kind of weird that you would get me out of going to prison only to attempt to kidnap me or kill me."

She pinched the bridge of her nose and a gust of wind blew against her again. "I know," she grumbled under her breath. She nudged him with her foot. "I'm not going to kill you, but this storm will. You have to come with me."

"What is your obsession with me?" he asked, raising an eyebrow. "Why are you following me around and trying to get me to go places with you?"

"Because I am an angel sent from God, and I'm here to recruit you," she told him with a sigh.

"Recruit me? Is this some kind of cult?" he scoffed.

"Oh my...no. It's not. It's honest work. I'm not even asking you to say yes or no to that right now, I just want you to get out of the cold, so I have a chance to ask you tomorrow. So please...get up and follow me."

Gabriel stared up at her for a moment, clearly weighing his options. "I don't know..."

Dani shifted on her feet before letting out a sigh. "Fine... but you made me do this," she muttered. "When you were in the seventh grade you stuck a grape up your nose because a girl you liked dared you to and you had to have it surgically removed."

Gabriel frowned and held up his hand to his nose. "How...how did you know that?"

"Because I've read a file on you before coming down here," she said.

"A file?" he asked.

"Yep," she grinned. "A file. Well, it's a small folder that has every important moment in your life from birth all the way up until now. I was given it and told not to mess this up. So, can you please get up and come with me? Even if you say no, I rather have helped you get out of the cold for one night."

Gabriel continued to stare at her for a moment before he nodded. "Fine, one night," he mumbled. "I'll stay with you one night. It's not because I want to do this, I just don't like the cold. Wasn't built for it."

"You really weren't," she muttered as she looked him over. "You're practically skin and bones."

"Being homeless will do that to you," he muttered. He got up and started to pack up his things. He glanced at her. "Do angels have apartments?" He wrapped the blanket around his shoulders before pulling his bag over his head.

"Technically no," she told him as she waited for him. Once he looked like he had everything she started walking with him. "But during our time on Earth a space is created to house us. It makes things easier, so we don't have to keep returning to Heaven." She looked down at him. "Do you believe that I'm an angel now?"

"I believe that you're crazy and somehow made a really calculated guess," he murmured He tugged the blanket tighter around his shoulder. "But if you kill me, you kill me. At this point I'm just wondering how far you'll go with this whole routine."

"It's not a routine," she muttered. "But don't worry, I'll find a way to show you who I am. Are you still hungry after that breakfast sandwich?"

"Starving," he mumbled.

"Okay, we'll order food as soon as we get there," she assured him. "And then we can talk."

Gabriel let out a groan and dropped his head back. He wasn't looking forward to that at all.

They walked the rest of the way to the apartment in silence. Gabriel wasn't sure if he was doing the right thing or not, but it clearly wasn't the first time he ever did anything questionable in his life. Plus, he wouldn't admit it out loud to Dani, but he was intrigued about her claims. There was something about her that tugged at him. It wasn't just because she was insane and thought she was an angel. Though, the fact that she knew what he did back in seventh grade was probably a big factor.

Dani led him into a seemingly abandoned building and up a set of stairs. She counted under her breath as she made her way down the hall and then stopped suddenly.

"This is it," she told him, looking over her shoulder with a grin.

He looked at the door. *Why do all the pretty ones have to be insane?* he thought. The door was practically rotting and looked like it would fall off the hinges if they tried to open it. He looked back at her. She was still smiling. "This is it?" he finally asked, pointing at it.

She nodded and turned back to the door. "I know it doesn't look like much but..." she turned the knob and pushed open the door.

Behind the rotting door was a small apartment. It was a studio with two beds, a couch, a table, a small kitchen, and a bathroom. It was bland but it served its purpose.

"What do you think?" she asked as she walked in.

Gabriel stared wide eyed as he slowly took the first step. He looked hesitant like he wasn't sure if it really was going to be there or not. "This place..."

"I know," she told him. "It definitely doesn't look like it belongs here. But that's the beauty of it. It hides us in plain sight."

Gabriel gripped the strap of his bag as he looked around. It wasn't anything spectacular but that didn't matter. "It's amazing," he said after a moment.

Dani raised an eyebrow as she looked at him. "You think it's amazing?" she asked.

Gabriel nodded slowly before moving to sit down on the bed. "I mean...it's not that much but it..." he looked at her and swallowed. "It looks just like the place I shared with my mom before she died."

Dani's face softened and she nodded slowly. "I see," she said quietly. "Have a seat and I'll get us some food."

Gabriel slowly walked back to the door and toed off his shoes before carefully slipping his bag and blanket from his shoulders. He walked back towards the middle of the room before sitting down. "Where are you going to order from?" he asked.

"Trust me, it's not a place you heard of," she told him. She walked to the small kitchen area and looked around. She sighed before pulling open the oven and seeing a bag of takeout in there. She pulled it out and opened it up.

The smell rose up out of the bag and she let out a quiet humming noise. It smelled so good. The food was one of the things that she missed the most about life on Earth. In her full angelic form, she didn't have to eat but while on Earth and in her human angelic form she was almost always starving.

"Food's here," she called as she carried the bag over to where Gabriel was sitting on the couch. "You'll love it."

"How did you get this?" he asked as took the bag from her.

Dani took the bag back and then pulled out her food before handing it back to him. "You know, I thought you got the gist of how things work with the apartment part. Everything in here is set up to have all my basic needs covered while I'm here on Earth. I assume they think you're staying with me because I have two beds. I never have two beds. Also, it is laid out like your old apartment."

"Are you saying this," he motioned around the room, "was all for me?"

Dani nodded as she started eating. "Every last bit of it. Surprised?"

Gabriel nodded slowly. "Definitely," he muttered. He looked back at her. "I think I'm starting to believe you because if this isn't real then I am having a very vivid hallucination."

Dani shook her head and went back to eating.

As they ate, she decided to speak up. "You know, you've done a lot in your life that I've been questioning. You seem to be a morally ambiguous person. You break the law, but you don't feel good about it. I've been trying to figure you out for a while, but I can't put my finger on it.

"I guess what I'm coming around to say is…you shouldn't be breaking the law for anything. It's not right and I don't understand why God wanted me to recruit you."

"Look, I know that what I've done is wrong," he told her as he twisted then twirled one of the chopsticks around his fingers. "Didn't you fight to have me go free because I did everything out of necessity?"

Dani let out a sigh and nodded. "I did say that, but those words were just that. Words. I didn't mean them. I said what I had to say to get you out. It's not what I felt though."

Gabriel looked down into his food. "Oh," he mumbled. "Then what do you feel?"

"I feel that even though you did what you did for the sake of survival doesn't mean that it wasn't wrong," she sighed. She took another bite of her food before setting the container in her lap. "You broke the law no matter how you turn it and look at it. It is something that you should be punished for."

She wondered if that was why God sent her to him. To punish him in a way. It wasn't her usual work, but she believed that she could do it.

Gabriel pulled his legs up onto the couch and looked like he was about to cry. "What do you think my punishment should be then?" he asked quietly, glancing to her.

Dani let out a soft sigh and shook her head. It wasn't why she was sent there, and she knew it. "It is not my job to punish those who have sinned. Your punishment will come in any way that God deems fit. He sometimes sends down angels like me for that kind of thing, or takes care of it himself."

Gabriel watched her for a moment, shaking his head. He couldn't believe that he was considering believing all of this. He was half expecting to wake up at any moment to some old drunk peeing on him again.

"You know, Gabriel," she said after a moment of silence, "sometimes you have to remember that there are people who have it worse than you and still don't stray from the path of light. They stay true to it and let their conscious guide them to the right answer. There is no excuse to breaking the law, even if it meant saving your life."

Gabriel shook his head. He didn't believe that. Sometimes breaking the law helped more than anyone could have imagined. "Why are you here then? What do you do?"

Dani smiled. "I'm glad you're starting to believe me," she laughed quietly. She was willing to let the conversation about right and wrong slip by. She said what she had to say and now it was Gabriel's turn to choose which path he wanted to take. "I'm here because I am assigned to souls who are looking for and need a miracle. It could be for anything and anyone, no matter their status in life. If they've uttered the words "I need a miracle" and actually needed it then they would be granted one."

"No matter what?"

Dani nodded with a small smile. "No matter what," she told him. It's a way of getting them closer to God in hopes that it would cleanse the world of evil."

Gabriel stared at her with a raised eyebrow. "That sounds incredibly fake," he mumbled.

"If you give me another night, I'll show you that it's not fake at all," she told him with a grin.

Gabriel thought about it for a moment before nodding.

"Fine, fine. I'll give you one more night. If you turn out to be a nutcase or I'm hallucinating all of this I'll be upset," he warned her, pointing his chopstick at her.

Dani held up her hand in a placating gesture. "I promise that this is all real and you are not hallucinating anything," she said. She turned back to her food and sighed as she saw the container was empty. So much for filling up for the night. She set it to the side and watched Gabriel as he ate. She still wasn't sure what God saw in him, but she was going to have to follow his instructions.

CHAPTER THREE

SHOW ME HOW

*T*he next few hours were spent with Gabriel sleeping. After they spent most of the night talking, he crawled into one of the beds, the one that he usually slept in when he lived in the look alike apartment. He told her to wake him up as soon as the sun started coming up.

When the time came though she was already up and working. She didn't even think about disturbing Gabriel. She knew that he needed his sleep just as much as he needed food. Maybe if she pumped him full of food and made sure he wasn't completely exhausted all the time she could get him back on the right path.

It was late afternoon when Gabriel finally woke up. He stretched out, hitting both ends of the small bed with his hands and feet. He turned over on his side and quickly shielded the light from his eyes. "What time is it?" he groaned. He pushed himself up, groaning as every muscle felt like it hurt.

"It's almost four," she told him as she was reading over a

file. She glanced up at him and laughed because his hair was stuck up in several places. She motioned with her hands towards her own hair. "Looks like you slept well."

Gabriel frowned and reached up. His thick hair was definitely all over the place. He groaned and tried to pat it down, but it wasn't going anywhere without a proper wash. He glanced towards the door that the bathroom was behind. "Does the shower work here?" he asked her.

"It definitely should," she told him. "I don't see why it wouldn't. If you put the clothes, you're wearing into the hamper they should come out clean and mended. Yours definitely need it."

Gabriel looked down at his jeans and t-shirt before looking back at up at her. "What's that supposed to mean?" he asked defensively.

Dani sighed and rubbed her head. "I mean, your clothes are holey and the last time you had a shower was probably at the jail house. It's not your fault that they're like that but they can be fixed. I didn't mean to cause any offense. I'm only observing."

Gabriel nodded slowly before getting up. He smoothed out his shirt before heading towards the bathroom. "I won't be long," he called over his shoulder.

As soon as he got into the shower he started to relax. The warm water eased his aching muscles and joints and he could feel the dirt and grime slowly sluicing off of him.

Usually he managed to catch a shower at a free gym or in a shelter, but it wasn't often enough, and he was almost never alone. Showering with a whole bunch of strangers quickly made it his least favourite thing to do.

Gabriel soon stepped out of the bathroom feeling more like himself than he had in years. His clothes were almost as good as new, his hair was smooth and manageable, and his breath probably didn't smell like everything he ate in the last few days. He tried to keep up on brushing his teeth while he could, but the cops had taken his toothbrush and seemed to have lost it along with what little bit of cash he had, and a few pairs of boxers.

Dani looked up and grinned when she saw him. He looked like a completely different man and while he was smiling, she saw adorable dimples on each of his cheeks. "Feeling better?" she asked.

Gabriel nodded quickly. "Yeah," he admitted. "I didn't know how much I needed...well any of that really."

"You're even looking like you're getting some of your colour back," she told him. She motioned him to the couch before standing up. "Have a seat, I'll make you something. In the meantime, you can read up on the first soul who needs a miracle."

Gabriel frowned and walked over to her. He grabbed the folder and looked at the name. "Seth Timberland?" he asked.

"Yeah, in that folder has all of the information we need on the guy," she told him. "We're going to be saving his soul tonight at approximately 3:47 AM."

"Oh," Gabriel muttered. He sat down and dropped the folder in his lap. He opened it and quickly went through all the pages. "I didn't know there would be homework."

Dani laughed as she started to pull things down from the cupboards. Everything she needed was at her fingertips. "It's a real pain to read them sometimes but it helps give us some kind of sense of what they truly need from us."

"Can't you just go to them and give them their miracle?" Gabriel asked. He laid down on the couch and started to read over the information.

"Well...yes," she said quietly. "But if we did that then the person might not learn from it or really feel it. In this case, Mr. Timberland wants to stay alive. He knows that he's close to death and he wants to stay alive just long enough to see his daughter's wedding. He's been on and off the streets...'

"So, are you just going to cure his cancer and let him go to his daughter's wedding?" Gabriel asked, looking up from the folder.

"No," Dani sighed. "Unfortunately, we can't do things like that. Well, not all the time at least. We're going to give him another year to live and it's going to be an easy year. He won't be in pain after today and will be well enough to even walk his daughter down the aisle."

Gabriel frowned and then turned back to reading. After a moment he sighed and lifted his head again. "How do you know if it worked?"

Dani walked over to the couch and leaned on the back of it to look down at him. "When you do it you see the different paths, the person can choose to take. Sometimes there are hundreds of paths that can be taken. After you do it though there is no real way of knowing if it helped or not. We're still spreading God's good will but not imposing his will on people."

"How do I fit into all of this?" he asked, tilting his head back to look up at her. "I can't perform miracles for people."

She wagged her finger. "That's not true," she told him. "In fact, people can perform miracles for others all the time. It's not always as grand as what I do, but they're still miracles. In this case though, you will have the same ability as me, bestowed upon you by God. That is if you choose to help."

He nodded slowly before going back to reading. "I think I actually know this guy," he said eventually. He looked at the picture attached to the file and studied it for a moment. "I think he's a drunk and he definitely does drugs. I've seen him buying from this guy Marty."

Dani looked at him and wondered if he understood it was those types of people that needed help the most. She shook her head and sighed. "We cannot pass judgement upon him, that is God's job. I have been sent here by him to help him. Just like I have been sent here for you."

"I don't need a miracle though," Gabriel told her. "I just...I just need a break."

Later that night Dani led Gabriel along the streets. "You'll get used to the feeling," she told him with a small laugh as he rubbed the middle of his chest. "I should have warned you sooner."

"That it would feel like my chest was about to set on fire...yeah, you should have," Gabriel muttered.

"I'll remember that for the next person I recruit," she teased. "In fact, at the end of all of this do you mind filling out a survey to explain how well I did. Anything to help me improve."

"Every one of them so far will be not satisfied," Gabriel muttered. He was still rubbing his chest and his eyes were screwed shut. "Why does it hurt so much?"

Dani sighed. "We're getting closer," she told him. "Do you recognize this area? If you know where he might be then we can find him sooner."

Gabriel looked around before nodding. "This way," he muttered. "He likes to hang around the bars and there's this one that gives out scraps to the homeless when they can. He usually ends up sleeping there."

He led her a few blocks down the street before stopping in front of the bar. The feeling in his chest was almost unbearable and he wanted it to go away. It made him feel like stripping off all his clothes and lying in the snow in an attempt to cool off. He didn't even think that would help.

In the alley they found him curled up, coughing under the thin blanket. Gabriel glanced at Dani. The old man looked like he was seconds away from death.

"We have to act quick," Dani whispered as she knelt down by his side. She then pressed a hand in the center of his chest. "Put your hand over mine," she told him. "Hurry."

Gabriel got on his knees next to her and quickly covered her hand with his. "Now what?"

Dani closed her eyes. "Now we say the prayer of miracles over him," she whispered. She pressed her hand harder against his chest. She could feel his heart fading fast. She started to whisper the prayer, the words lifting into the night and floating up to Heaven to be answered.

Gabriel felt lighter than air. It felt amazing. The words Dani spoke wrapped around him in an embrace and he tilted his head back, repeating the same words she did.

Dani jumped and looked at him. She hadn't expected him to catch on so quick. She shook her head and quickly continued.

When the prayer finished, she watched as two paths of life shot out from his soul. One where he got to go to his daughter's wedding, meet his new grandchild, and finally ending with him in a hospital bed surrounded by family, and the other was filled with more back alleys and various drug deals.

There was nothing she could do to persuade him either way. It was not her choice to make. She leaned down and pressed a kiss to his dirty forehead before pulling away.

Gabriel pulled his hand away and stood up. "That was amazing," he told her. "I feel...I feel...I feel alive," he finally got out. He held out his arms and spread them wide as he stared up at the night sky. "How come that felt so good?"

"Helping someone else always feels good," she told him. "I don't see why you're surprised."

Gabriel smiled at her before nodding. "I want to help you," he told her. He needed to. That feeling was amazing, and he wanted to feel it again.

CHAPTER FOUR

TO SAVE A SOUL

*A*fter their first soul the two started to work on other souls on the long list that Dani had to work through. Each week they performed two miracles. Gabriel would usually do one at the beginning of the week and then Dani would do the one at the end of the week.

One morning, a month after starting the work, Gabriel nudged her as they were eating breakfast. "I've got a question for you," he murmured around his spoon.

"I know your mother taught you table manners," Dani laughed, shoving his shoulder. "Why don't you take that spoon out of your mouth and say that again. I didn't catch even the slightest hint of it."

He rolled his eyes and pulled the spoon out of his mouth. He swallowed what food was left in his mouth before leaning against the table. "I have a question," he told her.

"Okay," Dani said slowly as she leaned against the table as well. She looked him over quickly, something she had taken a habit of doing every morning.

His health was improving, his colour was returning to

him, and it looked like he was even gaining weight. She was so happy to be able to help him and hoped that after all was said and done, he would use this opportunity to get his life back on track.

"How come we only do two miracles a week?" he asked. "I mean...I know you've got a stack up in the big house that's probably miles long. Wouldn't it be easier if we do...I don't know, multiple ones a day?"

Dani let out a sigh and looked down into her bowl. She pushed back her hair only to have it fall forward again. "As I'm sure you can already tell the effects of performing a miracle are quite addicting," she told him. She glanced up at him. "It can almost become like a drug."

That was another thing she was always looking out for with Gabriel. If he started showing any signs of being hooked, then she would have to find a way to cut him off before it got too bad.

In all honesty she was afraid that he was already slipping down that slope. When it was her turn to perform the miracle, he tried to do it and she had to push him away. She lied to him and told him that it was an advanced miracle.

He told her that he could handle it but eventually backed off.

"A drug?" Gabriel asked, raising an eyebrow. "Why does it matter? It's not like it's as bad as heroin or anything like that. In fact, you're helping people."

Dani sighed, rubbing a hand across her face. "Listen," she said quietly. "If someone becomes addicted to it then it becomes more about helping themselves and less about helping the person who actually needs it. Let me ask you this...how did you feel about people having large charity events to help the homeless."

Gabriel thought about it for a moment, stirring his cereal.

"I guess I felt like they didn't actually care," he mumbled. "They collected all that money, but it didn't seem to go to anything useful."

"That's because almost all of them did it for selfish reasons," she whispered. "If you are doing something to help yourself instead of helping the person who needs it then it almost nullifies the point. Don't you think?"

"You're right," Gabriel sighed quietly. "But I still don't think it's all that bad. I mean, I get where you're coming from but..."

Dani shook her head. "No," she said firmly. "There is no arguing this. There's also another danger lurking out there."

He rolled his eyes. Sometimes he hated how mysterious she tried to be. "And what is that danger?" he murmured.

"Every time a miracle is performed demons catch scent of it," she told him. "A scent of a miracle attracts them. They're always out there, watching and feeding on everything, they only come after one of us if someone tries to perform one and it doesn't work."

Gabriel dropped his head forward and groaned. "Christ sake, Dani," he said as he stood up. He took his bowl to the sink. "These are the things that you tell a guy before they start working with you." He turned to face her and leaned against the counter. "I want to make sure I got this straight. Demons are out there all the time and they eat...things?"

"People, animals, plants, cars, anything they can get their hands on really," she nodded.

"Okay, okay, and they get attracted to failed miracles."

"Oh, it's like candy to them. Or I guess a steak."

"And miracles can fail how?"

Dani rolled her eyes. "Well, in a few different ways. If you don't know the right words or you mess up, if you are too late, or if you found the wrong person," she explained.

He shook his head. He couldn't believe it. Soon he started pacing trying to rearrange all the new information. Suddenly he stopped and pointed at her. "Can you kill a demon?" he asked.

"I can," she smiled. "I don't know about you though. Angels are given special swords that can fight the things humans cannot see."

Gabriel frowned quickly. "What do you mean the things humans cannot see?" he asked.

She smirked. "We'll learn about all that in next week's lesson."

"I hate you," he mumbled. He stalked out of the kitchen and into the bathroom to get ready for the day.

Ever since Gabriel learned about the existence of demons, and other things that he could not see that Dani refused to talk to him about, he started to work on getting in shape. He took up running in the morning, then a quick stop at the gym, and then a few workouts that could be done at home.

It wasn't like they had much to do during the other days of the week. It got pretty boring just sitting around and doing nothing but reading files. Dani just kept producing them out of thin air. She claimed they were from her office, but he had no way of confirming that.

Of course, they talked a lot. They got along quite well with each other and created a rhythm that worked seamlessly.

Dani's favourite question was when Gabriel asked what Heaven was like. They were sitting on the couch leaning against each other as rain beat down on the window. She was a little caught off guard by the question but smiled, none-theless.

"Well, my part of it and your part of it are totally different," she told him, picking at a piece of fuzz on his sleeve.

"My part?" he asked, glancing up at her. "And what is my part?"

She smiled. "The part where humans go when they die," she told him. "There it is this amazing place with breathtaking views. You could do almost anything imaginable there. Almost all of your family will be there."

"My mom?" he asked, tilting his head to the side.

The question tugged on her heartstrings and she nodded. "Yeah, your mom will probably be there," she whispered. "And anyone else you could possibly imagine would be good enough to go there will be there."

Gabriel sighed and looked down. "So, not me?" he asked. It was supposed to sound like a joke, but it came out cracked and squeaky.

Dani rolled her eyes. "You're making up for a lot of things by helping me out down here."

He smiled and nudged her. "Now tell me about your side."

"Oh, you don't even want to hear about that particular Hell in Heaven," she groaned playfully.

They didn't stop talking that night and ended up falling asleep on the sofa together.

"Do you think I could fight a demon?" Gabriel asked one day.

Dani sighed and looked at him. "No," she said. "If you keep asking, I'll have to sic one on you."

"You wouldn't do that," he narrowed his eyes. "But I don't know if I would mind so much if I came face to face with one."

"Please don't say things like that," she muttered. She took a sip of her coffee as she settled back against the sofa.

Gabriel worried her almost every day about something

new. She thought he was going to get addicted to performing miracles, not that she was worried he was going to try to summon a demon. One time, she was certain he was trying to anger God by saying as many swear words he could think of and adding either God or Jesus to them.

"I'm just thinking out loud," he told her with a grin. "How big are they?"

"I don't know, I never saw one," she told him with a sigh. "Can you ask questions that aren't detrimental to your or my health?"

Gabriel raised an eyebrow. "Do you think they're even real? Has anyone seen them?"

"Well we all have a sword to fight them off so yes, I'm sure someone has seen them."

Later that day her and Gabriel were with a young woman on a pack bench. She was young but was stuck in an abusive marriage. Her miracle was a way out.

Dani had her hand pressed to her chest while Gabriel paced behind them. As she started to say the words Gabriel bumped his shoulder against hers.

She didn't open her eyes and her words didn't fault but she jolted again when he did the same thing.

As quickly as she could she finished up the prayer and then pressed a kiss to her forehead. "We'll leave you be," she whispered, squeezing her hand.

"Thank you," she whispered, looking at the both of them. In a few hours she would forget their faces and they would just become a distant memory.

Dani started stalking away and Gabriel was quick to follow. "I think it's been a week since I've done mine. Why don't we go find another one and I can do it really quick?"

She ducked down the alleyway which was a shortcut towards their apartment. She turned on him as soon as they were out of sight of everyone else. "What do you think you're doing?" she asked. "Do you think you're funny?"

He held his hands up and backed away. "I don't know what you're talking about," he said. "I was just asking to perform another miracle."

"Exactly!" she shouted.

A few people at the mouth of the alley turned but in the customary city fashion they all turned a blind eye to the fight.

"What do you mean exactly?" he asked, taking a step back.

She let out a frustrated growl. "I told you before that if someone does too many, they become addicted, and that is bad," she told him. "You're going down the wrong path my friend and I don't know if I'll be able to pull you back up if you do."

Gabriel rolled his eyes. "Oh, shut up," he muttered. "You don't know what you're talking about. I only want to help people."

"Then what were you doing earlier?" she asked, jabbing a finger against his chest. She held up a hand before he tried to explain himself. "I know what you were doing. You were trying to distract me so I wouldn't finish the prayer."

"Why would I do that?" he asked, raising an eyebrow quizzically.

She shook her head and jabbed another finger into his chest. He hit it away. "You want a demon summoned. I know what you're thinking, Gabriel. You can't let yourself get caught in situations like those."

"And why not?" he asked, crossing his arms over his chest. "I'm perfectly capable of handling myself. I have never been addicted to anything and if need be, I could handle a fight."

"With a demon?" she asked, eyes wide. She then started

laughing, shaking her head. "Oh my god. How can you be such an idiot?"

He glared at her. "I thought we weren't supposed to judge others?" he grumbled.

"Well you're pretty easy to read," she told him.

"I can handle myself, Dani," he assured her. "Even if a demon showed up, I would be able to hold out until you showed up."

Dani shook her head. "I don't think there is much holding out to do while fighting a demon, Gabe," she said quietly. She touched his arm gently. "You're still human. You can still get hurt. That's the last thing I want to happen to you."

Gabriel swallowed and looked away. He cleared his throat before nodding. "Fine, fine," he muttered. "I'm sorry. I'll try to be less reckless next time."

"Why don't you try not being reckless all the time," she told him with a grin. "See how far it gets you. I bet you'll live to see 99."

"I don't know," Gabriel smiled. "That sounds kind of boring. The adventure is in dying young." He started walking again, shoving his hands into his pockets.

Dani frowned as she watched him go before quickly moving to catch up. The words he spoke made her feel hollow inside.

CHAPTER FIVE

I'M LOSING MYSELF

That night Gabriel started getting antsy. He paced around the tiny apartment, huffing every so often. He even managed to walk into the furniture. The couch being the one he hit the most.

Dani took in a deep breath and told herself to be patient and that his boredom would pass soon. She hoped that it would pass into him sleeping and she wouldn't have to deal with him the rest of the night.

The pacing stopped and she smiled, laying her head back on the armrest of the couch. When she felt hot breath against her face, she opened her eyes and shoved Gabriel's face away. "What is wrong with you?" she finally asked. She sat up and let her hair fall around her face as she watched him.

"I'm bored," he groaned. "I want to go out. I haven't done anything fun since I've met you."

Dani frowned. "That is not true, Mr. Mendoza," she told him with a serious expression etched on her features.

"Having fun once in months does not count as having

fun,' he told her. "You and I both know that. So, don't start with that."

She rolled her eyes. "I wasn't talking about that," she muttered. "I was talking about the miracles. They're fun in their own way. Euphoric even."

He gave her a look.

She gave him one right back.

"I'm going out," he told her with a grin. "You know, to have fun and all of that. I need to stretch my legs."

She quirked an eyebrow. "I'm pretty sure you have paced about three miles since we got back this afternoon. Why don't you sit down and relax a little? We could play a card game?"

Gabriel shook his head and pushed away from the couch. His dark eyes were shining bright even in the low light of the room. "I'm going out for a few hours..." he called over his shoulder. He grabbed his jacket and was out the door. Before it could shut, he yelled, "Don't wait up!"

Gabriel walked down the street keeping an eye out for anyone who might need help. He knew of the chance of summoning a demon while performing a miracle on the wrong person was high, but he felt like he had a knack for it by now. He could tell who asked for one. He was sure of it.

After a few minutes he finally spotted a prostitute leaning against a wall smoking a cigarette. He walked over and offered her a smile. "Hello," he grinned, keeping his hands in his pockets. "I'm Gabriel."

She smirked and dropped her cigarette. "Oh, my, my, aren't you a handsome little devil," she rumbled. "What can I help you with?"

Gabriel kept the wide smile on his face. "Well, I was hoping I could help you," he told her. He leaned in close to whisper. He nearly choked on the strong mixture of cigarette smoke and perfume. "I can perform miracles."

She raised an eyebrow before looking him up and down. "You think you can really perform a miracle?" she asked. She let out a small laugh. "Why don't we find out over there? Unless you had somewhere specific in mind."

He shook his head quickly. "No, no," he said softly. "It can be done anywhere. Even right here."

"Oh, my poor boy," she laughed. "I don't think that's very smart. You don't want everyone else witnessing your...miracle, do you? Then they all would want a piece?"

"You're right," he whispered. He looked around before grabbing her hand. "Let's go over here."

Quickly he led her into the alley by where they were standing. She was laughing as he did and told him to slow down. "We've got all night baby," she told him. "Tell me, what do you like?"

Gabriel made a face before shaking his head. He pressed a hand to the center of her chest and started whispering. He felt the words swirling around him again, filling him with intense joy and happiness. It was like they tapped a part of him he hadn't felt since he was a kid.

"What are you doing?" she asked, frowning. She tried to push his hand off her chest. "What are you saying?" She pushed him back and broke the bond.

He felt his entire arm turn cold as he stumbled back. "I was performing a miracle. Please, let me continue," he whispered.

"What? I thought that was some weird sex thing. No," she told him firmly. "What does that even mean? Are you some psycho that gets his rocks off by killing prostitutes? Thinking you're all high and mighty."

Gabriel stared at her for a moment before shaking his

head. "Definitely not a sex thing," he muttered. "I wasn't even...I'm trying to get you out of this life."

"Get out of this life?" she asked. "Honey, I make more money than half the doctors in this country. I think my life is pretty good." She looked out towards the street before looking back at him.

"Please, let me just try," Gabriel told her.

She raised an eyebrow. "You want to do anything with me it will be $100 now and $50 for every hour after. Sorry, I'm not standing around here looking pretty for nothing."

He paled. "I don't have that kind of money," he told her. "Please."

"If someone says no, they mean no," his mother's voice spoke to him inside his head.

Gabriel shook the thought away. This was different. He was trying to help her. That's all. It was for her benefit. He needed to perform the miracle.

The prostitute froze and stared up into the air behind Gabriel's head. He frowned as a shadow came over him. "What- "

As he turned, he came face to face with a creature that he had never seen before.

"Run," he managed to get out before it screeched in his face. As it stopped, he could hear the clicking of heels running the opposite direction.

In the blink of an eye, the demon went to grab for Gabriel and he barely missed the giant claw by dropping to the ground.

He quickly crawled between its long tree like legs and scrambled to his feet on the other side of him. As he stood, he noticed that the demon already turned around to face him. He knew what he had to do. Keep the demon away from the people.

Gabriel stared up at the demon, taking all of it in. It was a large dark looking creature. It was at least eight feet tall, including the antlers on its head, and had a mix of fur and bark covering its entire body.

In an attempt to look like he could handle the situation he put his fists up and squared his shoulders. "Alright big guy, it's just you and me right now."

The demon roared and lunged towards him, easily knocking him against the wall. It started to move, and Gabriel grabbed around its foot and managed to trip it.

He then jumped to his feet and ran towards its torso. He kicked it as hard as he could and instantly regretted it. Pain shot up through his leg like a shock and he hopped away. It felt like he had just kicked a tree.

The demon quickly recovered and turned its dark icy stare towards him. It ran to him and slammed its shoulder into Gabriel's torso and rammed him into the wall.

Gabriel felt the stone break against his back, and he bit his lip to stop himself from crying out. The demon pulled away only to jam his shoulder into him again. The second time it felt like a rib had cracked.

As the demon pulled away a third time Gabriel wrapped his arms around his neck, so he was pulled with it. He jumped before his feet could leave the ground and then pulled as hard as he could down on the demon's head at the same time as slamming his knee into its face.

It stumbled back, making a whimpering noise but it didn't look like it was hurt too bad. Gabriel was just thankful that he didn't break his leg in the process, but its face was so far the only soft part he felt on it.

Instead of wasting time he moved forward and started to hit it against the face. He landed hit after hit until the creature swiped its clawed hand across his side. He gasped and stumbled to the side. He pressed his hand against where the claw got him, and he pulled it back to see blood coating his hand. He looked down to see it also quickly spreading across his shirt.

Before being able to examine it more he was hit with another blow which sent him flying down the alleyway. He landed hard, smacking his head against the ground, and blacked out for a few seconds.

What woke him up was hot liquid dripping on his face. He opened his eyes and saw that the demon was now over him. Gabriel swallowed hard and wondered if it was in this moment that people's lives flashed before their eyes or if it was the moment just after death.

The demon lurched its head forward and he moved faster than he ever had before to stop it from tearing off his face.

His fingers curled around both jaws and he pushed up against him as the mighty beast used all of its strength to press down upon him.

More saliva dripped onto his face followed by blood, as its teeth dug into his fingers and palm.

He quickly turned his head and squeezed his eyes shut as he pushed as hard as he could against the demon.

Not only could he hear his mother's voice telling him that he did something wrong again he could also hear Dani calling him an idiot.

"Hey idiot!" Dani's voice came again.

Gabriel's eyes shot open. In a puddle of saliva by his head he could see a bright light. He tilted his head back and his mouth hung open in shock.

Dani stood there in her angelic form. Her wings spread out wide, touching each wall of the alley and rising far above her head. In her hand was a sword which flames danced around.

"Why don't you pick on someone your own size," she taunted

The demon let out a piercing shrill and before Gabriel knew it the demon was off of him and running towards Dani.

CHAPTER SIX

SAVE ME

*D*ani had felt uneasy since Gabriel left the apartment. She didn't like how he just left like he did, dismissing her and barely giving her a moment to question what he was doing. She wouldn't have cared so much if she wasn't technically in charge of him.

She was sent to Earth to find him and to get him to see and understand what was happening in the world around him. She was charged with getting him to understand his part in it all. And he was something special too. She noticed as soon as they did their first miracle together. He was able to tap into the power right away and learned how to speak the language of the prayer within seconds.

That was something she'd never seen before and she was honestly a little afraid of it. A human having all that power was unheard of. She had wondered if that was why God had sent her down there.

Though, she wasn't sure if it was to find his weakness or merely protect him.

If she could go back to God in that second, she would tell

him it was impossible to do either so could she just keep him? If not as a partner, but rather as a friend?

He had frowned upon her, and he knew it. That's how he got away with so many things while she was around. But this wasn't going to be one of those times.

Dani climbed off the couch and grabbed her jacket. She really opened that she found Gabriel before he did something stupid.

As Dani was walking around the city, she felt the cold familiar chill of a demon entering the human plane. She swallowed hard and closed her eyes. If she concentrated enough, she would be able to tell where it was.

As demons moved about in the human realm, they left little ripples that were easy to follow if one knew how to read them. Fortunately, Dani knew how to read them. Unfortunately, she only studied them for a few weeks and gave up realizing that if she just did her job right, she wouldn't have to worry about demons.

Of course, that was when she was working alone and not with some lunatic who turned out to be an adrenaline junkie who didn't know how to follow simple instructions.

Was it her fault that this had happened? Possibly. She did tell him how to summon a demon. If she didn't do that then maybe, just maybe, there wouldn't be a demon plaguing the city right now.

She felt the ripples again and noticed that instead of rampaging through the city and devouring as many people as it could, the demon seemed to be staying in one spot. She started running towards the center of the ripples, feeling them roll over her like she wasn't even there but it still made her stomach queasy.

As she was rounding the corner, she found not only the demon, but also Gabriel fending the beast off with his bare hands. She stared at the scene for a few seconds. She didn't see any blood, there was a lot of saliva, the broken wall, and the demon on top of Gabriel inches away from his face.

It felt like her world was tipping to one side. She knew it was now or never. She held her hand above his before looking towards the demon and her friend. "Hey idiot!" she yelled but the two kept fighting.

She shook her head and whispered something before she changed into her full angelic form. Her hair flowed down to her waist, her wings spread out as far as she could get them, and her clothes changed to pristine white robes.

In her hands she held a long sword with flames licking up the blade of it. "Hey idiot!" she called again. A grin split her face when both the demon and Gabriel looked over.

She dragged the tip of her sword against the ground leaving scorch marks behind.

As the demon lunged at her she ran towards it. They met in the middle as two unmovable forces. The ground around them shook and the fight began.

Dani swung her sword, striking it in his chest. It got stuck in the bark. It stood up straight, bringing her and her sword with it before it shook them free.

She fell to the ground but quickly recovered as she ran towards it again. She landed blow after blow after blow. Each hit landing somewhere where there was a protective layer of tree bark it seemed.

The demon dodged one of her attacks and caught her off guard. It grabbed her by the throat and lifted her off the ground. Her legs kicked as she tried to wiggle out of the hold, but she knew that wasn't going to bring results.

With a furious yell she swung up her sword and hit it against a part of the demon's arm that wasn't bark and she fell to the ground. The demon looked down at its hand before letting a loud roar escape it before it spun in on itself and disappeared.

Dani quickly sat up, taking the severed demon hand off of her throat and tossed it to the side. "Gabe!" she called as she pushed herself up.

As she ran over to his still body, her heart stopping as the fear that she was too late flooded her system, she changed back into her human form. She scooped him up as quickly as she could, quickly assessing his injuries.

There were scratches covering his face and throat and she felt a cut on the back of his head as she cradled him against her chest. The biggest concern was the giant red spot blooming on his side that was only growing bigger. "I'll get you to the hospital," she whispered to him. "You just have to hold on. Okay? Just hold on."

She knew that Gabriel couldn't hear her, and she just gripped him to her chest as hard as she could before she ran out of the alleyway, tears streaming down her face. She didn't stop even as people yelled at her.

All around her people were standing and staring but as soon as a few of them could see the blood that now soaked her and was dripping onto the sidewalk they called for an ambulance.

Dani would have run all the way to the hospital if she didn't feel hands grabbing at her. She spun around, frustration flaring to life behind her green eyes. She was ready to fight anyone who dare try to hurt him again.

When she saw the flashing lights of the ambulance and it was paramedics that were stopping her and not some creature she broke down. She nodded her head and quickly handed Gabriel over before climbing into the back of the ambulance with them.

As they started driving, she squeezed her eyes shut and

shut out the rest of the world. All she could see was Gabriel's limp form.

She couldn't stop thinking how it was all her fault. She dragged Gabriel into it and allowed him to get hurt.

She wished that she had killed the demon instead of injuring it. It was the only time she had ever wished death on anything.

After spending two hours in the hospital waiting room, she was finally allowed back to see Gabriel. They had checked her over when they first arrived and asked her questions, but she couldn't tell them anything. Words couldn't escape her even if she wanted them to. It felt like her throat had closed up.

As she walked to Gabriel's room, she started to try to think about what she wanted to say to him. She had to say something to him. There were so many emotions swarming inside of her and she needed to get them out.

During her wait she had started to think about the situation and realized that it wasn't her fault at all. She told Gabriel not to do certain things and he went out and did both of those things.

She just wanted to know what he did and why.

Gabriel was sitting up on the hospital bed looking thoroughly beaten. His back was to her and she could see tons of scratch marks and cuts. Her mind went back to the broken wall she saw, and she winced.

"Gabe?" she asked quietly.

He spun around quickly and groaned as the stitches on his side tugged. "Dani," he whispered.

Relief flooded her and she rushed forward to give him a hug. "I'm so happy you're alive," she whispered into his shoulder before pulling away. She searched his face for any kind of answer she could find easily but found none. She cupped his cheek and pressed their foreheads together before pulling away. "What were you thinking?"

Gabriel looked down into his lap. "I wanted to give someone else a miracle," he whispered quietly. "I thought that if I did, it would be okay. I knew she needed one."

"But did she want one?" she asked, crossing her arms over her chest. "Because if she didn't want one then she was no one for you to touch."

"I was about to talk her into it when the demon appeared," he told her urgently. "I swear, I wasn't trying to summon it. I was just trying to save her."

Dani shook her head. "Gabe, not everyone can be saved. At least not by us," she told him. "God has a job too, you know."

Gabriel fell back onto the bed, ignoring the stinging pain of his back. "I know," he let out a small whine. "Believe me, I know."

"Really?" she asked. "Because it's starting to seem like you aren't understanding anything. I've told you not to go off book and that's exactly what you did. You may not have wanted to summon a demon, but you ended up doing it anyway. You're too reckless for this job. Too childish."

"Please," Gabriel whispered, "don't say that."

Dani shook her head. "It's the truth. I don't know why you insist on turning around and disobeying me every chance you get."

"You're not my keeper," he said as he avoided meeting her gaze. "I don't answer to you."

"Yes, you do," she told him. "God sent me to recruit you and train you. I am in charge. I'm sorry that you can't accept that, but it's the truth."

Gabriel sat up again, gritting his teeth together. "You're

the one that chased after me, I didn't even want to do this stupid thing."

"So, you would have rather died out on the streets than work with me?" she asked incuriously.

He glared up at her, his hands clenching into fists despite the stitches that pulled at his skin. "A thousand times over."

Dani let out a hollow sounding laugh and looked down. "Right," she muttered. "Then I guess I'll just leave. Good luck living on the streets again."

And without another word she walked out of the hospital room.

CHAPTER SEVEN

I'M SORRY

*G*abriel sat in the hospital bed and stared at the door long after Dani had left. He was furious with how she responded to what happened. She had no right to come in and get angry at him. He was just doing the job he was forced into.

It wasn't even something he wanted to do. He would have been fine spending the rest of his days on the streets wasting away. She didn't give up though and found ways to manipulate him into doing her work for her.

If anything, she was the worst of the two. It was her fault that he was laying here in the hospital bed at all. She made him work, made him put his body through giving miracles, something that she knew was addictive.

Plus, he didn't even do anything wrong. He knew that the prostitute needed a miracle. It shouldn't matter if she wanted it or not. She should have just accepted it and not have demanded money from him. The demon wouldn't have shown up if she let him perform the miracle for her.

The walls of the room started to feel like they were

closing in on him the more he thought about it. He squeezed his eyes shut but he could still feel the pressure.

All he wanted to do was help. What was so wrong with that? Wasn't that what God had wanted from him? What Dani wanted from him? He couldn't tell what was right and what was wrong anymore.

Why was he only allowed to save some people and not others? What made any one person more special than someone else? Was it just because they asked for the help?

None of the answers were coming to him and he quickly pushed himself out of the bed. He knew one thing for sure, he couldn't stay in this room for another second.

He gathered up his clothes off the foot of the bed before he started to change into them. They were still covered in his blood and torn to shreds but they were all he had.

As stealthily as he could, he made his way out of the hospital room and through the corridors. He wasn't sure if he would be stopped if he was seen, surely the people who brought him in had called the police as well, but he wasn't going to risk it. If he made it outside, he would be free to do as he pleased.

The night wasn't as cold as he remembered it being. Spring was right around the corner. It would be easier to transition back to street life during the warmer weather.

He walked down the street a bit and wondered if he should go back to the apartment or not. He looked around and spotted a few guys standing outside smoking. He walked over to them and offered them each a smile. "Mind if I bum a smoke off of ya?" he asked, scratching the back of his head.

One of the men looked down at him before sighing. "Yeah," he muttered. "I guess I'm the cigarette man for today."

"Sorry," he laughed, motioning to the scratching on his

face and neck, "it's been a rough day." He put the cigarette between his lips and nodded towards the man's lighter.

"I can tell," he laughed as he lit it for him. He held out another one to him. "For the road."

"Thank you," he laughed before sticking it behind his ear. He brushed his fingers against the long strands and sighed.

Dani had offered to cut it for him, but it was just before they were going out on a job. By the time they were finished they were both too hyped up to even remember.

He sighed softly and shook his head. He didn't want to think about her or anything else.

He inhaled the smoke and felt the burn of it as he travelled down into his lungs. As he exhaled it swirled into the night, mixing with the pollution of the city.

Gabriel decided not to head back to the apartment. He wasn't ready to see Dani yet and he wasn't even sure if she wanted to see him at all. He knew he needed to clear his head if he wanted to go home otherwise, he would just end up starting another argument.

As he was walking, he kept circling around the thought of whether or not he was right in doing what he did. It wasn't something he wanted to think about. Honestly, all he wanted to do was put it behind him.

But he didn't feel like he was in the wrong. How could he be? All he was doing was helping. If helping someone was wrong, then why should he even bother? How could he get in trouble for doing both good and wrong? He felt cheated.

As he walked along the street he decided to duck into a shop. He had some pocket change that would hopefully get him something to snack on while he thought about what his next move should be.

He looked around for a while before looking at how

much he had. There was nothing that he could get except for a packet of gum.

A part of him told him to just steal it. No one would care. Even if he didn't, he probably would get stopped by the store clerk on the way out. He reached for a bag of chips, looking around. As soon as his fingers touched the bag his mother's voice came to him.

"My baby boy. Don't ever do anything that would put your heart at risk. You're worth more than what everyone else thinks of you."

Gabriel closed his eyes and let out a small sigh. "Mom," he sighed softly. "It doesn't matter. Right or wrong."

"I love you, my baby boy."

His hand started shaking and he quickly withdrew it. He shoved his hands in his pockets and started to head out of the door. He smiled at the store clerk. "Sorry, realized I forgot all my money at home," he told him. "Thanks, have a great night."

"Wait," he called. "Are you hungry?"

Gabriel frowned before looking down. "A little, yeah," he admitted. "It's fine though."

"Choose something," he told him. "I'll pay for the rest of it," he assured him. "Go."

He was surprised by the act of kindness and went back to grab the bag of chips. He brought them to the counter before taking out his wallet. He was a dollar short. "I'm sorry."

The store clerk looked at the food before looking at him. He shook his head and pulled out his own wallet. He took Gabriel's dollar before handing him a ten. "There," he said. "For when you need to eat again. Thank you for coming."

Gabriel stared down at the money before looking back up at him. "I- "

He held up his hand. "I won't hear anything else about it," he told him. "Please, come back any time you're hungry."

"Thank you," he said softly, nodding his head towards him. He slipped the money into his wallet before walking out of the store. He looked down at the bag of chips he was given and then looked out into the city.

Guilt overwhelmed him and tears started to spill down his cheeks. He didn't know why he was crying, maybe it was because he had yelled at his friend and told her that he would rather die instead of working with her.

With that thought and the sudden feeling in his chest he tucked away his bag of chips into his jacket and started running back towards the apartment.

He didn't care if people saw and thought it was suspicious or if they thought he was weird. He needed to apologize to her as quickly as he could. He really was an idiot.

Gabriel didn't stop running until he was standing in front of the apartment. He panted hard as he bent over, resting his hands on his knees. When he stopped seeing spots he quickly headed inside and jogged up the rickety stairs. "Dani!" he called. "Dani! I'm sorry!"

He pushed open the door and frowned when he saw that it was empty. He walked over to the bathroom and knocked on the door. "Dani? Are you in there?" he called. "I'm sorry."

There was no answer.

Gabriel looked around the apartment and ran a anxious hand through his hair. He had no idea where she could be.

CHAPTER EIGHT

I WAS TRYING TO

*D*ani hadn't realized how upset she would be at having an argument with Gabriel. As she made her way home her gut wrenched and she wanted to go back and apologize to him, to tell him that she was wrong, but she knew she wasn't wrong. They had rules set in place for a reason and a whole lot more people could have gotten hurt. Gabriel could have gotten himself or an innocent bystander killed.

She didn't understand why he couldn't listen to anything she ever told him. He always had to be the best. She was hoping that almost being killed for his stupid actions would have changed that for him, but it didn't.

Instead they both reacted badly and ended up hurting each other. But Gabriel's words cut really deep. She didn't want to think about losing him as a friend or him losing his life. She would do anything to stop that from happening.

She shouldered her way into the apartment and let out a deep sigh. It felt so empty already without Gabe there. She wished she didn't get angry like she had. She could have kept her head about it all as well. The fight wasn't just Gabriel's fault.

She took off her jacket and headed towards the bathroom so she could drop the clothes in the hamper

When she walked back out again, she found a note sitting on the counter. She frowned and walked over to it, looking around to make sure no one had followed her in.

The note read:

"Nicolas Mendoza's soul is being tainted by the demon you injured. Head there now before he's taken over. Don't waste time. -G"

Dani frowned as she read the note again. She didn't understand. How was she supposed to take care of this? It wasn't her jurisdiction.

She clasped her hands together and bowed her head. *"Dear Lord, heed my prayer…"*

"I am listening child."

"What should I do? I don't know how to save Nicolas Mendoza as you have asked. Please, guide me."

There was a pause before he answered. *"Do what you know is best in your heart. I cannot guide you on this one. This is your own personal judgment. I trust you."*

The connection between her and the Lord was cut off and she lifted her head. On the note now was an address which she could find Nicolas Mendoza at.

She hurried around the apartment and gathered her things before heading out, leaving the note on the counter.

Dani knew that she should probably try to get in contact with Gabriel, but she didn't think he could handle receiving news about his father. Especially with him not taking things as seriously as they needed to be. He probably wouldn't even believe her if she told him.

So, she set out on her own to find Nicolas and defeat the

demon. It would be easy. She already fought the demon once, what harm would it be to battle him for a second time?

If God trusted her judgement and this was what she thought, then she would be fine.

Right?

It took her hours to find the place on the address. It was outside of the city and hidden deep within acres of woods. As she approached the building, she could feel the ripples of the demon moving around and she shivered.

She didn't like that feeling at all. She changed into her full angelic form and pulled her sword from the sheath. It would draw the demon out and away from Nicolas if he hadn't already been taken over.

She wasn't sure what to even do in that case. Would she have to kill Gabriel's father?

That would be something that Gabriel would definitely never forgive her for. She felt the ground moving and she looked up through the trees, seeing the demon charging for her.

At least now she knew it wasn't inside of Nicolas yet.

The demon screeched and pushed trees out of its way as it barrelled through the forest. When it got close enough it pulled one out of the ground, roots and all and threw it at her.

Dani screamed at the top of her lungs and sliced through the tree with her sword. It caught on fire almost instantly and fell to the ground. She glanced over her shoulder and saw the flame quickly spreading.

She would worry about that later. She pushed herself forward, sword raised for an attack. She stuck down but was blocked and then swatted away like a fly. She slammed into a tree and fell to the ground. She looked back towards the flames and saw that they were spreading quickly.

She had to move the fight out of the forest. Before she could get up the demon walked over to her and stomped her into the ground. She felt all the air leave her lungs and she gasped to take a breath.

As she struggled, she lifted her sword and stabbed it as hard as she could through the demon's leg. It howled and stumbled back towards the flames.

That was when Dani got the idea that maybe the flames could kill it. She grabbed the hilt of her sword and yanked it out as hard as she could.

It caused the already unbalanced demon to stumble back and then she stabbed it in its stomach, driving it towards the flames. When she pulled out the sword it was the final push that was needed.

The demon fell back into the flames and landed with a loud thump.

Dani watched it for a moment before turning and heading towards the house. She had to make sure that Nicolas was okay.

Suddenly the ground became to shake again as she was about halfway to the house and she stopped to turn around. The demon looked larger and was currently on fire. It started to run towards Dani, its teeth barred.

Dani swallowed hard and held up her sword. She didn't really see herself defeating the demon, but she wasn't going to just lie down and take whatever destruction it had in mind. She let out a hellish yell as she prepared for the demon to strike.

CHAPTER NINE

SAVE YOU

*G*abriel started to worry after Dani didn't show up at the apartment after twenty minutes. He had changed and got a new set of clothes, grabbed something more to eat, shaved, and yet she never returned home. Gabriel's heart began to race as a rush of emotions fell over him. These feelings were different and unlike any he had felt before. He was concerned for Dani, but it was over-whelming. Gabriel needed to find her, in that moment he felt untethered.

He started to search through the apartment for anything she could have left behind to indicate where she had gone and only then did, he see the note on the counter.

At seeing his father's name, he froze. Why was anything after his father? How did the demon even know where his father lived? He didn't even know that information.

He had to guess that that was where Dani had run off to. He didn't understand why she ran off without him. Then again, he seemed useless against the demon not even hours ago. Why would he be of any help now?

He quickly shook his head. He couldn't think like that. Two people he knew were now in danger and they needed his help.

After snagging the note he headed out of the apartment. He knew where the place was. It was somewhere his father used to always take him when he was younger. They would go fishing and spend long weekends there.

All before his dad left him and his mother.

He quickly pushed the anger down and started to head out of the city. He hoped that he wasn't already too late but there a heavy stone settling in the pit of his stomach.

Gabriel arrived a half hour later and saw a forest full of flames and the demon from earlier, but this time it was so tall its head bobbed above the trees.

He started to run towards the scene but then he heard a loud scream that could only belong to Dani. His heart nearly leapt out of his throat and he started to run faster. He wasn't going to let anything happen to her.

Not now.

Flames jumped around him, but he kept going. He didn't care if he got burned, all he had to do was get to Dani and potentially his father before the demon did.

When he reached the edge of the woods though he saw Dani battling with the demon. She was slashing her sword at its arms as it swung towards her. He wanted to run up and help but he didn't see an opportunity to jump in with what he had.

"Dani!" he shouted to her, hoping that her knowing he was there would be enough to help her go on.

Dani growled and shot a look towards him. She paled. He couldn't be here. He would get even more hurt or get killed. "Run!" she called to him. Each attack she blocked was harder than the last and she felt her heels digging into the ground.

The demon lifted his fist and slammed it against her. She tried to block but it smashed her into the ground.

Gabriel swallowed hard as he watched her get smashed into the ground. He started to run forward but then the demon disappeared. He paused and looked around before shaking his head. He needed to check on Dani before worrying about where the demon disappeared off to.

He fell down by her side and pressed a hand to her cheek. "Dani," he whispered, tapping her cheek gently. "Dani. Please wake up."

Dani barely opened her eyes as she looked up at him. "Save...save your father," she managed to choke out. "He needs you."

Gabriel looked up and that was when he saw his father walking out of the cabin. Except, instead of brown eyes that matched his own all he saw was a black film covering them.

"Gabriel," Nicolas said, swaying as he walked towards him. He held out his hand. "Gabriel. I have a secret I need to tell you." His head twisted to the side and his eyes were suddenly clear again. "Run!" He twitched and his eyes were black again. "I never loved you Gabriel. I never once loved you."

Gabriel squeezed his eyes shut. That was one thing he was never sure about. His father's love. It had plagued him for years after he left, and it was even worse after his mother died. "No!" he cried, shaking his head violently.

"I never loved you or your mother," he said. His body went rigid and then twitched again. "Gabriel, please," he begged. "Run. I don't want to hurt you."

"Stop it!" Gabriel shouted, balling his hands into fists.

"You were a mistake. Not even your mother wanted you. I told her to drop you off at the fire station and let them take

64

care of you. All you ever did was cry. No one wanted you around."

Each taunt and insult felt like a dagger stabbing into his chest. It felt like something cold and hard was forming in his chest and at any moment he would explode.

"I wished you were never born, Gabriel," he taunted, getting closer to him. "I know you wish the same."

Gabriel let out a loud angry yell and a beam of light shot into the sky, blinding them all.

Rain broke through the clouds and wind started to build up, blowing them both from side to side. The flames behind them started to diminish and sizzle.

Nicolas blinked a few times before looking around. "What happened?" he asked. His eyes were back to normal and he looked weak. He spotted Gabriel and gasped.

Gabriel knelt next to Nicolas and Dani, sharp silver wings protruding from his back and a sword with ice crystals swarming around it was stabbed into the ground. When he looked up and the whites of his eyes looked frosted over.

CHAPTER TEN

PLEASE FORGIVE ME

*D*ani slowly sat up as she was regaining her strength. She stared at Gabriel, her eyes traveling from his eyes to his large wings all the way down to his sword. She took in deep breath before letting it out slowly. "How did you do that?" she asked, reaching out to gently stroke his wing. The feathers were soft to the touch.

Gabriel looked at her and shook his head. "I don't know," he admitted. He looked to his father. He studied him a moment before looking at Dani. "The demon has escaped. We have to find it and get rid of it before it decides it's going to hurt anyone else."

Dani nodded quickly. "Look, Gabe, I'm sorry," she said softly. "I shouldn't have yelled at you; I shouldn't have run off to fight this demon alone. I should have told you that it was going after your father. I should have known that I wouldn't be strong enough to do this on my own."

Gabriel shook his head and helped her to her feet. "You could have done it on your own but sometimes you just need a little extra help from a friend," he said with a smile. "Now come on. We have a demon to slay together."

Dani nodded and squeezed his hand tightly. "Yes, we do," she whispered.

The ground began to shake again, and they looked up to see the demon towering over the house now.

Dani looked at Gabriel. "I think every time he gets hurt; he gets bigger. I think we need to really get him this time. If we don't, I don't know what will happen."

Gabriel nodded and then looked at his father. "Get inside," he told him. "You should be safer there. Can you make it there on your own?"

Nicolas looked at the demon before looking into the house. "I think I can," he said. He swallowed hard and looked over at his son again before he shook his head. "Stay safe."

Gabriel gave him a soft smile before turning back to Dani. "Let's get this guy," he laughed. He pushed off the ground and was in the air in seconds. "Get his limbs! I'll get everything else!"

Dani nodded and started to fly towards the demon.

In the air it was easier to dodge the demon's attacks. Gabriel didn't understand how he magically grew wings or how he suddenly knew how to use them, but at the moment he wasn't going to question it.

The demon swung towards Gabriel and he spun out of the way and sliced at its fingers. He pumped his wings harder heading straight towards the demon's head. He knew that was where he managed to hurt the other demon when they had first encountered it.

Dani sped towards its legs. She weaved between its legs, hacking at every part of its body that wasn't covered in bark. She had found out too late that that was its natural armour.

Gabriel felt his wings getting heavier and heavier as the

rain poured down on him, but he wasn't going to stop until the demon was down on the ground and dead. He swung his sword above his head as he got close to its face. As he pulled it down it froze the rain it touched instantly, turning them into shards of ice. He plunged the sword deep into the demon's neck as the ice shards needled into its chest.

The demon staggered with each passing blow and its movements grew slower and weaker. Gabriel saw this and stopped beating his wings. He stabbed his sword into the demon's chest and let his weight pull the sword down through his body.

When it got stuck, he pressed his feet against the flesh and pulled the sword out with great effort. He pushed off and flew away from the demon, darting towards the open area. "Dani! It's going down!"

Dani saw its feet staggering and she quickly flew towards Gabriel. Together they watched as the demon swayed, staggered, and then fell to the Earth. In seconds it disappeared into puff of black smoke.

Slowly they both flew to the ground and Dani fell into his side as soon as her feet touched the ground.

They both changed out of their angelic forms, Dani on purpose because she felt too weak to be able to hold onto it for too much longer, and Gabriel by accident because he didn't know how to control the shift.

He held onto Dani as he walked inside and found his father sitting at the counter with his gun in hand and his eyes wide.

"Did you get him?" Nicolas asked, before dropping his gaze to Dani. "Is she okay?"

Gabriel nodded. "We just…need to rest for a little bit," he told him. "The demon is gone. Do you mind if we sleep in the guest room?"

Nicolas nodded slowly. "Of course, of course," he told him. "Let me get a change of clothes for you two."

Gabriel pulled Dani to the bed and set her down. "Think you can change by yourself or do you need me to help you?" he asked.

Dani nodded. "I'll be fine," she murmured.

Gabriel nodded and pressed a kiss to her forehead before grabbing the clothes his father offered him. He went to the bathroom and changed and jumped a little when he saw Nicolas standing right outside the door.

"So...since when have you had wings?" he asked.

"Since a half hour ago," Gabriel told him with a grin. He sighed and pushed past him and started towards the guest bedroom. He paused at the door and looked at him. "I'll see you in the morning," he whispered.

Nicolas nodded. "I'll be here," he assured him. "I'll even make breakfast for you two."

Gabriel was utterly shocked as he knelt before God. He thought he had seen it all when he grew wings and fought against one of Satan's strongest demons but now, he was in the presence of God.

"My Lord," Dani started, keeping her head bowed, "I thank you for helping us and giving us the tools to find the right path. Without you we would have been lost."

God shook his head and laughed lowly. "It is not me you have to thank but yourself. You used what I gave you wisely. I am happy to announce that both of your mishaps and sins have been cleared."

Dani looked up quickly before looking at Gabriel. "Really?" she asked.

Gabriel glanced up but it felt like something was pushing on him to look down. He closed his eyes. "What does that mean, My Lord?" he asked.

"It means that you can go back to living your normal life and Dani Harp can move up the angelic hierarchy."

"I don't want to," they both said at the same time. They shared a amused look with each other.

"My Lord," Dani said, giving Gabriel a small nod. She understood what he wanted without him even saying a word. "I was hoping that I could stay on Earth and Gabriel can help me perform miracles all throughout the world."

God looked between the two. He knew what was in their hearts, but he still must hear it from them. "Is that what you wish, Gabriel?" he asked gently.

Gabriel nodded quickly. "Yes sir," he said and then he quickly shook his head. "I mean...yes, My Lord."

Another chuckle escaped God and he smiled. "Then my dear boy, you will keep your wings and your powers to give miracles where they are needed. You two will have to travel together and do twice the work." He gave a look to Dani who blushed.

"Yes, My Lord," she said softly. "I think together we can overcome it."

"Very well then," God smiled. "You two are dismissed. Just in time for your first assignment too."

Gabriel frowned. That was fast. "What is it My Lord?"

"Take some time off and recover," he told them. "You need your rest just as we all do."

Dani grinned and stood up. "We'll take Sunday," she joked. "Thank you again, My Lord."

Together they walked out of God's worship room and made their way to the door that led to Earth.

Dani swiped her card and the light flashed red. She glanced at Gabriel with red cheeks. "I'm sorry," she muttered. She quickly swiped it again. "This doesn't always happen."

Gabriel rolled his eyes and took the card from her. "Sure,

it doesn't," he said with a wink before swiping it for her. The light flashed green.

"Show off," she muttered. She glanced at the keypad before smiling. "How do you feel about Hawaii?"

"Oh, I was thinking of something more like Greece."

Dani grinned and punched in the code for Greece. "Perfect."

EPILOGUE

*G*abriel had packed a small bag of clothes along with some fishing gear. He stood near the door, hesitating to leave. He looked at Dani and offered her a smile. "Are you sure you'll be alright while I'm gone?" he asked her. "I mean, you've gotten used to having another set of hands around here. I don't want you to get sloppy and mess up and I was hoping the last demon we slain would remain the last demon we slain."

Dani rolled her eyes. "I swear to God I will pick you up and throw you out of this place myself if you don't leave right now," she told him. "I don't care if you're helpful or not."

Gabriel gave her a look. "Now, now. You know not to use the Lord's name in vain," he told her. "I doubt he would like to hear you say that."

"He hasn't smote me yet," she told him. She turned him around and started to push him towards the door. "Get out of here. I know what you're doing."

"No, you don't," Gabriel mumbled under his breath,

pushing his feet against the ground like a small child. "I'm not even doing anything."

"Exactly, the one thing you should be doing is getting out of this house," she told him. She pulled open the door and shoved him out. "And I don't want you back here until you smell disgusting and have at least three fish for dinner."

"We literally have a heavenly fridge!" he called, letting out a laugh. "Why do you need me to bring food home?"

"Why else would you be fishing?" she asked. "Now go, get out of my hair for a while." She shut the door and then locked it.

Gabriel stared up at the old abandoned house and let out a sigh. It was falling apart on the outside but looked amazing on the inside. He sighed and shook his head before stepping forward.

THE FLIGHT back home took longer than he expected but he was glad to be off of the plane. Ever since he started flying, he hated airplanes. They were too bumpy and full of people. He preferred the open air and feeling the wind on his face.

Dani had told him that if they were caught flying then their wings would be clipped for a few months until their feathers grew back, so he stuck to taking the more traditional route.

AN HOUR later he was standing in front of the cabin door. He was nervous to knock. Him and his father had been talking on the phone on and off ever since they killed the demon and prevented his possession and when his father suggested he come down for a long weekend Dani had practically forced him out, assuring him that everything would be fine.

He wasn't sure if it was because she wanted him to get close to his father again or if she wanted to have a weekend to herself after the months of constantly being around each other. He wouldn't blame her if it was the latter. He knew how hard it was to live with him sometimes.

The young man took a deep breath in before slowly letting it out. He knocked on the door and waited for his father to answer.

Nicolas pulled open the door and grinned. "Welcome home," he said and pulled him into a hug.

Gabriel went stiff as he was hugged but slowly eased into it. They weren't on the best terms yet. This trip was about getting to know each other again and opening up about everything. He wasn't sure if he was actually ready to do that, but he figured it would be better than not know anything at all.

When the demon had taken Nicolas over and spoke Gabriel's deepest fears, he wasn't able to handle it. He still woke up from nightmares about it and would in turn wake up Dani.

They would spend hours talking about what happened and she would help ease him back to sleep. He didn't know how he could express the amount of gratitude he had for everything she had done for him since they met, but he was hoping to find out one day.

"Dani told me I'm not allowed to come back without fish," he told Nicolas as he pulled away. "So…"

"We better not eat anything that we catch," Nicolas laughed softly. "Come on. Let's get your stuff settled in the guest room. Then I think we can crack open a few cold ones and build a fire."

"No fishing today?" he asked, raising an eyebrow.

"My boy," he laughed, clapping him on the back, "I'm an

74

old man. If I go out there this close to night, I won't be able to steer us back to the dock."

"I can do it," Gabriel told him.

Nicolas shook his head. "No, not after what you did to my boat the last time. We couldn't go fishing for the rest of the summer."

Gabriel gave him a wry look as the memories of that day washed over him. "I was seven and Mom told you not to let me steer the boat," he told him. "And we could fish from the dock, you didn't want to. You told me that all the small fish swam by the dock because they drank all my pee."

"And it's still true to this day," his father nodded sagely.

Gabriel rolled his eyes and went to put his things away.

THE NEXT DAY they sat out on the boat together in the middle of the lake. Gabriel flicked his line into the water and watched the bobber floating in the distance.

"Can- " Gabriel started.

"I- " Nicolas said as the same time as Gabriel. "You go first."

Gabriel sighed and looked down at his rod. "Why did you leave?" he asked, glancing back at him.

Nicolas laughed. "Starting with the easy questions huh?" he chuckled. He ran his fingers through his hair and pushed it back. "It's complicated."

"Don't give me that," he told him. "I want actual answers. Please."

Nicolas nodded and looked down. He reached around and grabbed a beer from the cooler. "Well...when I was a younger man, I got angry more often then I should have. I did my best to keep it to a minimum around you guys but eventually I started losing my temper more and more." He looked at Gabriel and sighed. He could see the pain behind his eyes. "I didn't do it because I wanted to be away from you, I did it because I wanted you guys to be away from me."

"What does that even mean?" Gabriel groaned.

"It means that I was turning into someone I wasn't, and I didn't like that," he whispered. "I was afraid I was going to hurt you or your mother. I explained to her what was going on and what I was doing, and she was supposed to explain it to you...but I don't think she ever found the right words to do so. I loved you and still love you every single day. I hope one day you could find it in your heart to forgive me and love me back."

Gabriel glanced at him and caught his eye. He gave a small nod before turning back to his line. "I'm sure we can work on it together."

The sun shone brightly on their backs and they continued fishing without another word.

It wasn't all repaired, but it was a start, and one that they had decided to embark upon together. Somewhere in the breeze he could hear God's chuckle. Gabriel smiled as a fish swirled and took the bobber under.

GABRIEL'S THOUGHTS drifted to Dani, and how much she had come to mean to him in the short time they have known each other. She was responsible for this chance to reconnect with his father, but more importantly, the reconnection to himself and the man he was always meant to be. He could not wait to get back home to her.

Thank You for Reading!

Don't forget to sign up for
Mind Flow Publishing & Production LLC's Newsletter @
www.mindflowpublishingproduction.com

Email us for autographed or additional paperback copies @
mindflowpubpro@gmail.com

Other Titles Also Available Include:
Mental Interlude—Poetry
The Mary B Chronicles 1- 4—Fiction
Journey to Living (Kindle Only)—Inspirational
Simple Complexity—Poetry
Spoken From The Heart—Poetry
Dreams Do Come True (Kindle Only)—Fiction
Charisma's Homecoming—Fiction
For Her Love—Fiction
Falling In Love With Poetry—Poetry
A Chance at Love—Contemporary Romance

Available Through:
Amazon
Barnes & Noble
Kindle

Coming Soon

What would you do if one day while at work-study, you learned you were a princess?

Elle is your normal college freshman, raised by a single mom, trying hard to get an education…and stay on her own two feet. One day while working in the library a mysterious stranger appears asking for materials relating to a small little country she had never heard of.

What happens next is a whirlwind adventure of one woman's journey of reconnecting with her father, and adjusting to the life of a royal… did I mention that she is supposed to find a husband as well? And all of this is taking place on a reality show designed to help the country get to know their young ruler.

Additional Upcoming Titles Include:

Freedom In The Cage Series—Fiction
Flint
Steel
Brick
Stone
Royalty—Romantic Comedy
Finding Kate—Suspense Thriller

Upcoming Titles Will Be Available Through:
Amazon
Barnes & Noble
Kindle
Apple iBooks
Kobo

ABOUT THE AUTHOR

Although I'm still considered new to the publishing world, I have hit the ground running full speed ahead. In my first year, I was signed to Mind Flow Publishing & Production LLC, and I have published a total of 6 books. I have earned Amazon's Best Sellers Top 100 orange banner. My works are spread across several genres such as; Poetry, Inspirational, Urban Fiction and Christian Fiction. I will be trying my hand at cozy mysteries, romance, and suspense thrillers. My love for writing started when I was about 12, writing poetry and writing speeches for various oratorical contests. Inspiration for my craft is pulled from my own life experiences, as well as others. I have been featured on several podcasts, as well as Up and Coming Authors Newsletters. When I'm not writing, I love to design shadowboxes, and create personalized greeting cards. I have released my 3rd poetry book (Spoken from the Heart) in August 2019. Some of my current books available are The Mary B Chronicles 1 - 4, Mental Interlude, and Journey to Living, Simple Complexity, Dreams Do Come True, Spoken from the Heart, For Her Love and Charisma's Homecoming. All of which are available on Amazon and www.mindflowpublishingproduction.com.

www.ingramcontent.com/pod-product-compliance
Lightning Source LLC
Chambersburg PA
CBHW072039170626
46811CB00008B/3109